that 17th hat

written by Trevor Eissler   illustrated by Marloes de Vries

For Ellie.
"I'm siiiiick."
"What's wrong, Ellie?"
"My feelings hurt."

Written by Trevor Eissler.
Illustrated by Marloes de Vries.
Designed by Bobby George & June George.

Cataloging-in-Publication Data

Eissler, Trevor
de Vries, Marloes
George, June
George, Bobby

Includes 29 illustrations
1. Montessori Learning 2. Verbal—Learning 3. Language—fluency and flexibility
4. Learning—Real world 5. Children's fiction
FIC E EIs 371.392 Ei 2011
ISBN: 978-0-9835558-1-0

JUNE BOOKS

www.junebooks.com

Printed in the USA

"I would love to find a new hat today. A perfect hat," Mom said with a smile. "You never know when there might be a special occasion."

"What's a perfect hat?" asked Wyatt Walcott.

"I'll show you! But first, who is hungry for lunch? Follow me!" called Mom.

Amelia Ann ordered wonton soup and milk.
Wyatt Walcott ordered moo goo gai pan and orange juice.
Lorenzo Luke ordered spicy chicken and iced tea.
Mom ordered Mongolian beef, an egg roll, and coffee.

When the delicious meal was finished, they set out to look for a perfect hat.

It started to rain.
And then it poured!
Of course, no one had
remembered to bring an umbrella.
And no one had a hat.

"We're all getting wet!" they laughed.
"If we had perfect hats we'd all be dry,"
thought Wyatt Walcott to himself.

"Oh no. Look!" Mom said.
"That sad little puppy is getting soaked, too.
I wonder where its owner is?
Oh well. Hurry children! Let's find a hat store!"

"Bat."

"Cat."

"Fat."

"Drat!"

7

"Hat!"

They burst through the door and gazed up
at the colorful collection of hats on the wall.

Wyatt Walcott walked right up to the store owner and said,
"If I had seventeen hats, just imagine that!"

Mom chose a bright orange hat from the shelf
and carefully positioned it on her head.
"If I wore a **turban**," she said,
"I would live in India, far, far away."

Choosing another hat, she said,
"If I wore a **toque**,
I would cook banana flambe."

*toque is pronounced *toke*

"If I wore a **beret**, I'd stroll around Paris, and then Marseille."

* buh RAY

Wyatt Walcott spied a helmet with a clear visor in the corner of the store. "If I wore an **astronaut helmet,** I would blast off into space."

Meanwhile, Mom showed Amelia Ann
how to tie a sun bonnet around her chin.
"My **bonnet**!" Amelia declared.
"No. Sunburn. On. Face."

Lorenzo Luke found a hat he liked.
"If I wore a **jockey cap**, I'd yell 'Giddyup!'
and win the Kentucky Derby race."

15

The store clerk handed an interesting hat
to Amelia Ann for her to try on.
He said, "If you wore a **fez**, you would live
in colorful Morocco!"

"If Amelia wore a **hard hat**,
she would drive a backhoe."

"If she wore a **sombrero**, she'd say, 'Hola, amigo!'"

"My **baseball cap**!" Amelia squealed.
"I. Hit. Home. Run."

"If I wore a **policeman's hat**, I would carry handcuffs, a holster, and a gun."

"When I was twenty-one, I wore a
mortarboard for college graduation."

"If you wore a **top hat**,
we would ballroom dance
and hear the cheers."

"If I wore a **keffiyeh**, sand from the Arabian desert could not blow into my eyes, my mouth, my nose, my ears."

* kuh FEE uh

23

"If you each wore **ushankas**, the freezing
Russian winter would not make you shiver."

*oosh AN kuh

24

"If I wore a **cowboy hat,** I'd yell 'Yeehaw!' and herd cattle across the Colorado river."

"These hats are all fun to wear," laughed Mom.
"But I don't have enough money to buy them!"

"We'll have to be content with our own hair on top of our heads!
Our own curly, straight, wavy, twisting, turning, crazy, long, medium,
short, brown, blonde, black, red, purple, wonderful hair."

"I think Amelia likes that one," said Wyatt Walcott.
Amelia Ann wanted to buy a hat.
"Well, I do have enough money to buy that floppy hat," said Mom.

"Let's make a run for it so we don't get wet!"

Amelia Ann didn't mind getting wet.

Where is Amelia?

"You found the perfect hat," whispered Mom.

31

To segregate by age…breaks the bonds of social life, deprives it of nourishment.
-Maria Montessori

A note to Parents:

That 17th Hat highlights some of the fascinating educational principles found in Montessori schools. One of the core principles is the importance of a mixed-age environment. The three-year age grouping of a Montessori classroom allows students to interact as a family, a community—a group of individuals across the age spectrum with a variety of interests, skills, needs, and abilities. Children work together and learn from each other. Younger children observe role models, leaders, and mentors. Older children reinforce their own learning by teaching younger classmates. They learn how to respect the contributions of younger children, while practicing how to manage and cultivate their classroom communities.

Another core principle of Montessori education is to ensure that students are immersed in a delicious verbal environment. Although children get plenty of "cat" and "hat" in their early years, it is important that they hear the complex sounds and meanings of words such as "bonnet" and "mortarboard," or even "keffiyeh" and "ushanka." The child's brain is a sponge for language. Just by being within earshot of older family members, young children learn an entirely new "foreign" language (their own) prior to setting foot in a classroom! The Montessori teacher builds on this eagerness for language by encouraging students to communicate with their classmates. And to intrigue the ear of her students, the Montessori teacher purposefully incorporates complex, scientific, and descriptive words from across the breadth of the human vocabulary into her own speaking.

If you find these Montessori principles intriguing, you may be interested in visiting your local public or private Montessori school to see for yourself. Simply ask to observe a classroom.

We have to conclude that scientific words are best taught to children between the ages of three and six; not in a mechanical way, of course, but in conjunction with the objects concerned, or in the course of their explorations, so that their vocabulary keeps pace with their experiences.
-Maria Montessori